MIDNIGHT in the CEMETERY

A Spooky Search-and-Find Alphabet Book

By CHERYL HARNESS

ILLUSTRATED BY
ROBIN BRICKMAN

Simon & Schuster Books for Young Readers

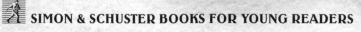 SIMON & SCHUSTER BOOKS FOR YOUNG READERS

An imprint of Simon & Schuster Children's Publishing Division

1230 Avenue of the Americas, New York, New York 10020

Text copyright © 1999 by Cheryl Harness

Illustrations copyright © 1999 by Robin Brickman

All rights reserved including the right of reproduction in whole or in part in any form.

SIMON & SCHUSTER BOOKS FOR YOUNG READERS is a trademark of Simon & Schuster.

Book design by Paul Zakris. The text for this book is set in 17-point Lo Type.

Printed in Hong Kong

10 9 8 7 6 5 4 3 2 1

LIBRARY OF CONGRESS CATALOGING-IN-PUBLICATION DATA

Harness, Cheryl.

Midnight in the cemetery: a spooky search-and-find alphabet book / by Cheryl Harness ;

illustrated by Robin Brickman. — 1st ed.

p.   cm.

Summary: An alphabet book, featuring collage art, in which ghosts

scare away two children searching for treasure in a graveyard.

ISBN 0-689-80873-9 (hardcover)

[1. Ghosts—Fiction. 2. Cemeteries—Fiction. 3. Buried treasure—Fiction.

4. Alphabet. 5. Stories in rhyme.]

I. Brickman, Robin, ill. II. Title.

PZ8.3.H218Mi 1999

[E]—dc21   97-34552   CIP   AC

**For Jared and Caleb,
safe and sound at home.**

–R. B.

A note from the illustrator:

I created the illustrations by cutting, painting, sculpting, and then gluing
pieces of watercolor paper together. There are no found objects or real or
preserved specimens in the artwork. With the exception of an occasional use
of wire, human hair, and paper I pulled from a fallen and abandoned wasp's nest,
the illustrations consist only of painted paper and glue.

Angels watch o'er silent sleepers,
Restless souls, and midnight creepers.
For some are awake in the autumn night
As the amber moon rises, round and bright.

Briars and brambles grow all around
This oogly-boogly burial ground,
Where black bats swoop without a sound
And a bandit's treasure might be found!

Buried under crumbling stones,
Are bodies and bugs, secrets and bones.

17 April 1765

Alice Alpine
Artist

Abe
Acorn
Aug. 1 1889

Abe Bean
Departed
and no longer
seen

In Memory
of
CALLA DEAR
Departed
in her last year

B.C.
Remember
~ me ~

B.C. DEB

Departed

It's midnight in the cemetery.
That's the time and place most scary
When graveyard cats are stealthy, stalking.
So why are children out there walking,
Clutching candles, barely talking?

Both of them were double-dog-dared
By big boys who said, "Don't be scared!
Hunt for an X and dig behind it!
Dig down down down until you find it:
Doubloons and diamonds—nothing gory,
Just deadman's gold—like in the story."

The story is of evil old Ed,
Who wanted his treasure buried next to his head.
And here is what his epitaph said:
No GOLD IS HERE, ONLY OLD ED,
WHO ONCE WAS ALIVE, BUT NOW IS DEAD.
At the edge of the graveyard, by a gnarled elm tree,
A child finds the X! "Come look and see!"

Forlorn funeral flowers shiver lightly;
The children's fingers tremble slightly.
Excitement lights up each child's face.
Fantastic! They have found the place!

They poke their shovels in the grubby ground . . .

ELFENEA

12

and BANG! The air is full of sound!
Ghastly ghosts swirl all around!
A gang of gray ghouls gasps and groans—
Dead Ed explodes from his granite stone!

13

"HA HA HA! Hey, kids! It's me!"
He hollers down from up high in the tree.
"I'm here to haunt you, hoping to be
The most horrible has-been you'll ever see!

"I'm not in your imagination!
I'll turn you to ice with no hesitation.
Ignorant insects! Impolite! ICK!
Take my gold, will you? You make me SICK!"

The kids' hearts jerk like jumping beans,
Their legs turn to jelly inside their jeans.
When spooks pop up like jacks-in-the-box,
They just about jump clear out of their socks!

Ed swoops like a kite: "I'm the **KING OF FEAR!**
Keep away from my gold!
KEEP AWAY FROM HERE!"
The kids bolt and kick like kangaroos.
Oh no! One trips on the tips of his shoes!

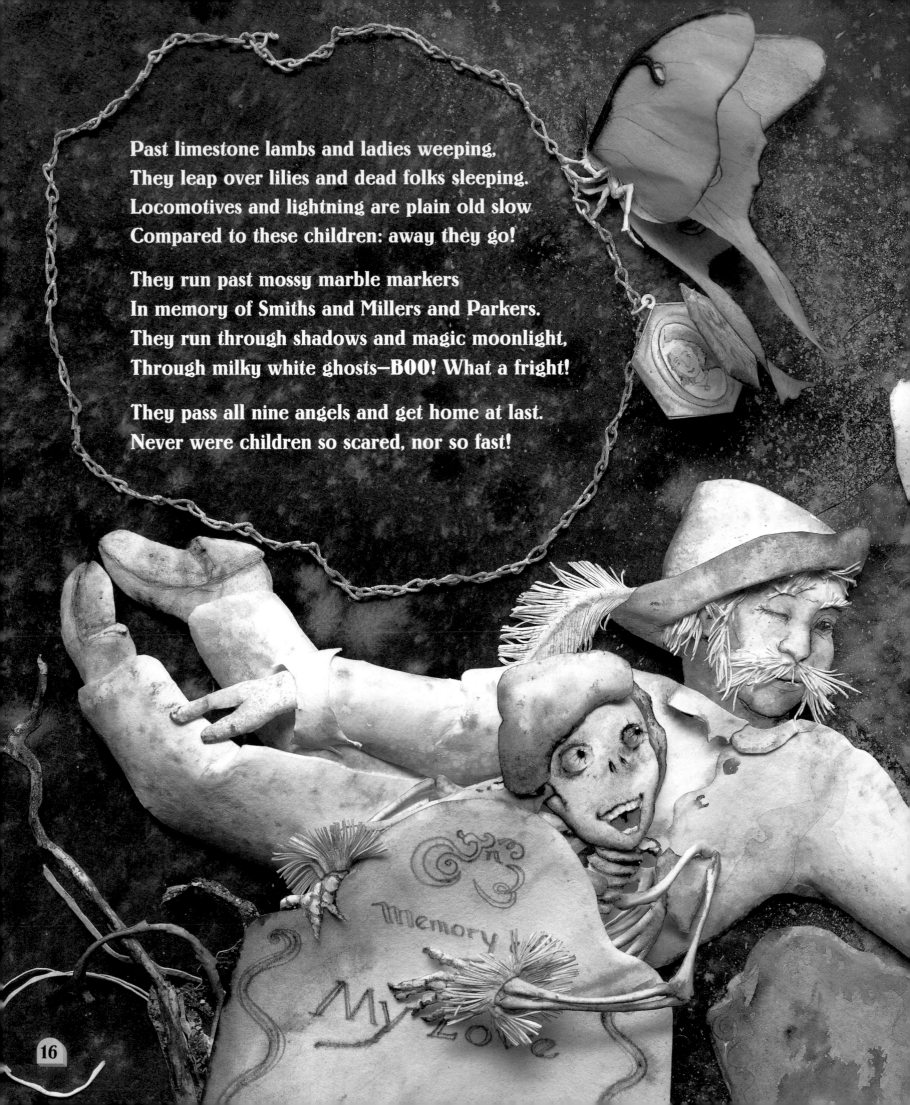

Past limestone lambs and ladies weeping,
They leap over lilies and dead folks sleeping.
Locomotives and lightning are plain old slow
Compared to these children: away they go!

They run past mossy marble markers
In memory of Smiths and Millers and Parkers.
They run through shadows and magic moonlight,
Through milky white ghosts—**BOO!** What a fright!

They pass all nine angels and get home at last.
Never were children so scared, nor so fast!

Then the noise of nasty nonsense fills the nippy night
As those nutty, no-good ghosts all natter with delight.

How odd and out of the ordinary,
This October night in the cemetery!
"Okay, friends," Dead Ed calls out,
"it's only one o'clock.
We've got hours to kill before it's day:
I say it's time to rock!"

(A PARTY!)
A parade of pale poltergeists promenade
And proudly brag about the noises they've made.
Ghosts dance the polka and play peek-a-boo,
Poke their partners and say, "Guess whooooo?"

A quartet of spooks plays a lively quadrille,
Quick on their pipes and fiddles until
The ghost of Dead Ed shouts, "Quit it! Be still!
The East's getting light. It's time to get quiet.
We're making such racket, we sound like a riot!

"We taught those rascals it's rude to come 'round
A graveyard at night to dig in the ground.
'Twas a night to remember and not to repeat!
They ran like rabbits with rockets for feet!

"We scared 'em good and sent 'em scootin'!
Well done, Spooks! But, sure as shootin',
When they're older, they'll think it's funny
To send littler kids here, searchin' for money!"

Ed sinks in the soil, like an elevator,
Saying, "Sweet dreams, Spooks! Be seein' you later."

They take one last look and drop out of sight,
Past toadstools, turtles, and mouse tunnels tight,
Down to their tombs and so ends the night.
Just in time for the morning light.

Up above: the umbrella of sky;
Down below: all the dead ones lie.
Under dry leaves and lacy ferns,
Under gravestones and marble-white urns,

Under the vine-covered mausoleum,
Sleep the ghosts, where no one can see 'em.
Their bones are as white as vanilla ice cream.
Sometimes they hear vampires' voices SCREAM!
(But that's only when they have a bad dream.)

When wild wind whistles in the weeping willows,
Wide-awake children put their heads under pillows.
"We won't pass those angels again," they say.
"Tomorrow, and after, we'll walk another way."

So if you should go where X marks the spot,
Don't dig for treasure, believe this or not:

It's been two yards down for many a year—
yellow gold, diamonds, and plenty of fear!

It's deep in the dead zone for safekeeping.
There's zero chance of taking it from Ed, who's
only sleeping!

It's morning in the cemetery
And nothing is so very scary.
Birds sing, the sun shines bright,
And tombstones glitter pearly white.

You'll find the following objects on the pages indicated. Numbers in parentheses tell how many such objects are hidden in the art (e.g. "angels (8)" under "pages 4-5" means there are eight angels tucked into those pages). Some are very easy to find, others are so tricky that even the illustrator forgot where they were! Happy hunting!

pages 4-5; A, B, C
Abe, Acorn, acorns (2), Alice, Alpine, angels (8), ant, April, Artist, Aug., barbed wire, bats (3), birch tree, blackberries (2), book, bookmark, bow, bugs (2), bushes, church, clouds
EXTRA CHALLENGE: crypt

pages 6-7; C, D
Calla, candles (2), cats (3), chains (2), children (2), circles (How many can you find? You should be able to spot at least 6 and maybe as many as 15.), clock, clover, cobweb, cocoon, coin, Coyote, cracks, cricket, Dear, Deb, Departed (3), diamonds (2), Drake
EXTRA CHALLENGE: calipers

pages 8-9; D, E
daddy longlegs, daisies (2), Dan, Days, dragonfly, drum, Drummer, drumsticks (2), Ed, Edna, egg shells, eight, elbows (3), Elfenea, elm tree, eyes (15 or more)

pages 10-11; F, G
face, feather, ferns, fingers, flame, flowers (3), foot, frog, glass, Gold, grass, grasshopper, gravestone, ground, grub
EXTRA CHALLENGES: fungi (2), ground beetle

pages 12-13; G
ghosts and ghouls (5), gravestones (3)

pages 14-15; H, I, J, K
hair, Hal, handkerchief, hands (10), hat, heads (How many can you find? You should be able to spot at least 10 and maybe as many as 17.), headstones (9), Here, hornet, Ice, inchworm, initials (2), jar, jawbones, jeans, jewelry, juggler, keys (2), kink, knots (4)
EXTRA CHALLENGE: iris

pages 16-17; L, M, N

lady, lamb, legs (How many can you find? You should be able to spot at least 8 and maybe as many as 21.), links, lips, locket, Lon, Love, luna moth, Mago, Marker, markings, Memory (2), Miller, mouse, mouths (7), My, necklace, noses (5)
EXTRA CHALLENGE: lyre

pages 18-19; N, O

necktie, nest, Nolly, noose, nostrils (How many can you find? You should be able to spot at least 9 and maybe as many as 29 or more.), octagon, one, Oona, owl
EXTRA CHALLENGES: obelisk, orchid

pages 20-21; P, Q

pair of angels, pants (5 pairs), parade, party, Peanut, pear, peekaboo, pipe, pirate, pointing fingers (4), puzzle, quartet, question mark
EXTRA CHALLENGE: panpipes

pages 22-23; R, S, T

R, rat, rest, ribbon, ribcage, rocks (3), S, scroll, seal, shadows, shoes (3), skeletons (2), skull, Sleep, snail, spider, spiral, spoon, stars (2), sticks (2), T (2), tail, To, toadstools (6), tree trunk, turtles (2)

pages 24-25; U, V

umbrella, unicorn, V, valentine, vault, vest, vines, Virgil
EXTRA CHALLENGES: ukulele, urn, vole

pages 26-27; W, X, Y, Z

watch, whiskers, whistle, worms (3), X, Y, yo-yo, zigzag, zipper, zodiac (partial)
EXTRA CHALLENGES: W, weevil, yarn, Z